TWO WEEK RESERVE:
NO RENEWAL

DATE DUE

~~HHT~~			

CHILD

Aladdin
and His Wonderful
Lamp

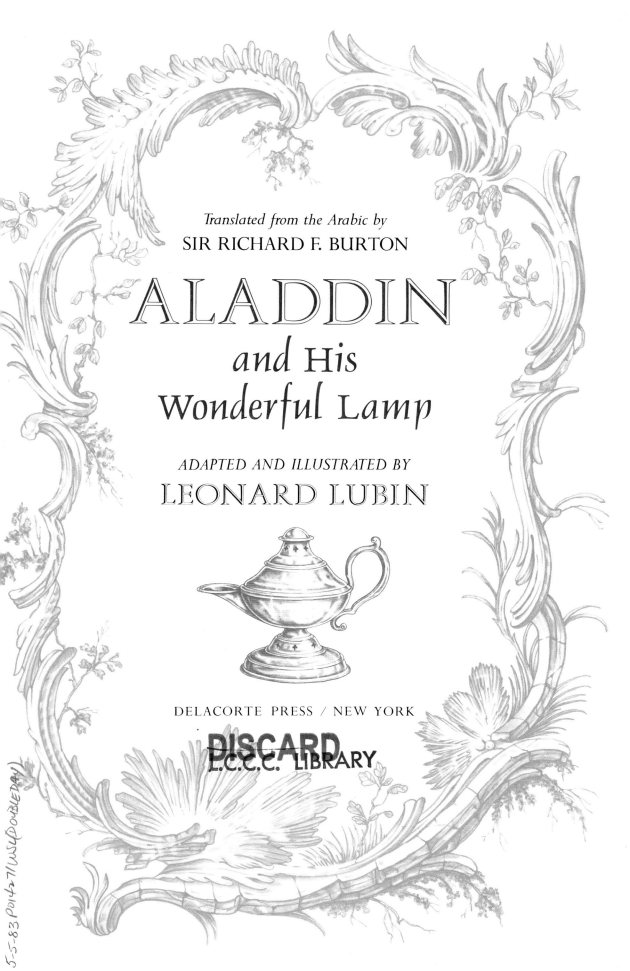

Translated from the Arabic by
SIR RICHARD F. BURTON

ALADDIN
and His
Wonderful Lamp

ADAPTED AND ILLUSTRATED BY

LEONARD LUBIN

DELACORTE PRESS / NEW YORK

Published by
Delacorte Press
1 Dag Hammarskjold Plaza
New York, N.Y. 10017

Manufactured in the United States of America
First printing
Designed by Barbara G. Hennessy

Library of Congress Cataloging in Publication Data

Aladdin.   English.
Aladdin and his wonderful lamp.

Translation of: Aladdin.
Summary: A poor tailor's lazy son finds a magic lamp
and uses it to win the hand of a beautiful princess.
[1. Fairy tales.   2. Folklore, Arab]   I. Burton,
Richard Francis, Sir, 1821–1890.   II. Lubin, Leonard B., ill.   III. Title.
PZ8.A34   1982   398.2'2   82-70308
ISBN 0-440-00302-4   AACR2
ISBN 0-440-00304-0 (lib. bdg.)

FOR PETER HAND

Aladdin
and His Wonderful
Lamp

NCE UPON A TIME, THERE DWELT in a city of China, a poor tailor who had one son, called Aladdin. When the boy reached his tenth year, his father wished to teach him his trade; and took the lad into his shop. But as Aladdin was disobedient and lazy, and preferred to play with the gutter boys, he would not sit in the shop for a single day. No, he would wait for his father to leave, then run off with other rascals and low companions of his age. Scoldings and punishments were of no avail, nor as his parents hoped, did he care to learn any other trade.

Presently due to worry and frustration, the tailor sickened and died. Aladdin's bad behavior continued, and indeed, seeing himself freed from the curses and beatings of his father, he increased in his idleness.

His mother sold the shop and took to spinning cotton, and by this weary task she fed herself and her good-for-nothing son. So time passed until the youth had reached his fifteenth year.

One day as Aladdin was idling about, a Wizard came up and stood gazing upon him. Now this Wizard, a Moorman from Inner Morocco, was a powerful Magician who could overturn mountains and read the heavens. By his conjuring and stargazing he had learnt of Aladdin, and so had traveled to China and sought him out.

"O my son, art thou the child of such-a-one the tailor?" he asked.

The lad answered, "Yes, my lord, but 'tis long since he died."

The Wizard, hearing these words, threw his arms about the boy and began kissing him, weeping all the while.

Aladdin was greatly surprised and asked, "What causes thee to weep, my lord, and how did thou come to know my father?"

"How canst thou question me such," replied the Moor in a sad voice, "after informing me that thy father, my brother, is dead! I've traveled far, and rejoiced in the hope of looking upon him once more and talking over the past. Now thou hast informed me of his death."

Presently the Moorman, having calmed himself, put his hand into his purse, and pulling out ten gold pieces, gave them to Aladdin, asking, "O my child, where is thy house and where dwells thy mother?"

Aladdin arose and pointed the way. The Wizard then said, "O my son, take the money and give it to thy mother with my greetings, and tell her that thy father's brother has come from his exile and on the morrow will visit her."

Thereupon Aladdin kissed the Magician's hand and joyfully ran home at full speed.

His mother was surprised at seeing him run in, as he never came around except at mealtimes. "O my mother," the lad exclaimed in his delight, "I give the glad news of mine uncle, who sends his greetings!"

"O my son," she replied, "it seems thou mockest me! Who is this uncle and how came he to be?"

Aladdin then told her of all that had transpired. "O my son," she sighed, "I wish that thou indeed had an uncle, but I am not aware that thou hast any."

The next morning the Moroccan Magician fared forth and made his way to the house of Aladdin. Bowing low, the Moorman greeted his sister-in-law, then he began to shed copious tears, asking her, "Where be the place whereon my brother used to sit?" Entering the house, he was shown the tailor's armchair. Going up to it, he kissed the floor, crying, "Ah, how unhappy and luckless is my lot, now that I have lost thee, O my brother!" And after much continued weeping and wailing he swooned away in an excess of grief.

Aladdin's mother was convinced of his sincerity, and so raising him from the floor, asked, "What gain is there in upsetting thyself so?"

Being consoled and regaining calm, the Magician told them of how he had left China forty years before, of his wordly travels

and settling in the Moroccan interior, and finally of his overwhelming desire to see his brother once again. "The day before yesterday," he continued, "while wandering about the city, I beheld my brother's son, Aladdin, playing in the street. The moment I saw him my soul joyfully informed me that he was my very nephew. But when he told me of the dear one's demise, I nearly fainted of grief and disappointment. However, I am consoled by the sight of Aladdin, for as they say, 'whoso leaveth issue is not wholly dead.' "

Turning to Aladdin, he asked, "O my son, what hast thou learned in the way of work, and by what means dost thou earn a livelihood?"

The lad was embarrassed and hung his head.

His mother spoke out: "How indeed! By the Gods, he knows nothing at all, a child so disagreeably wicked as this I never yet saw, no, never! All day long he idles away his time with the other good-for-nothings, and I must spin cotton night and day so that we may have food to eat. O my brother-in-law, being a woman of many years, I no longer have the strength to work, but I must provide him with daily bread, when it is I who should be provided for!"

Hearing this, the Moorman asked Aladdin, "Why is this, O son of my brother, that thou behavest in such a shameful manner? Surely there is some profession or craft which may please thee? Choose one, and I will establish and aid thee in it with all I can."

Aladdin kept silent and made no reply, by which the Magician

knew that the boy wanted no other occupation save that of a scapegrace-vagabond life. He said to him, "Very well then, since thou apparently dislikest the thought of learning a craft, I will open thee a merchant's shop and thou shalt buy and sell, and be well known in the city."

Now when Aladdin heard of his uncle's intention of making him a merchant and gentleman, he was exceedingly happy, for he knew that such folk dress handsomely and dine well. He looked at the Magician, smiling, and thanked him. The Wizard then said, "Tomorrow I will take thee to a bazaar and purchase a fine suit of clothes for thee, and will look for a store for thee and keep my word." The Moorman thereupon took leave, promising to return the next morning.

The following day the Magician took Aladdin by the hand and fared forth to the bazaar. They entered a clothier's shop and called for a suit of the most sumptuous kind. The apparel was donned and paid for, and they took their leave. Once outside, Aladdin kissed his uncle's hand and thanked him for his favors.

As they trudged about the Merchants' Bazaar, the Magician diverted Aladdin by showing him the market and its sellings and buyings. Then he led him forth and showed him the city with all the pleasant sights therein.

Soon they left the city gate and the Moroccan took to promenading with Aladdin amongst the gardens, pointing out the fine parks and marvelous pavilions. They passed from garden to gar-

den until they left all behind them and reached the base of a high and barren hill.

Exhausted, the boy asked the Moor, "O uncle mine, where are we going? Let us turn back."

Said the Moor, "No, my son, this is the right path, for we are going to look at a garden to which the others are naught." Then the Magician fell to telling Aladdin wondrous tales, lies as well as truths, until they reached the intended site.

"O son of my brother," the Magician exclaimed, "sit thee down and take thy rest, after which go and seek some wood chips and dry sticks with which we may kindle a fire. Then I will show thee things beyond belief and of which no one else has enjoyed."

Now, when the lad heard these words, he longed to see what his uncle was about to do. So, forgetting his fatigue, he immediately began gathering chips and sticks until the Moroccan said to him, "Enough, O son of my brother."

The Magician kindled the fire, then took out of his breast pocket a small casket from which he poured a quantity of powdered incense into the flames. Then he fumigated, producing whirling plumes of smoke, and conjured, muttering words and phrases none might understand. After much quaking of the earth and bellowings of thunder amidst thick forbidding gloom, the ground split apart, revealing a marble slab wherein was fixed a copper ring.

Aladdin became so frightened that he tried to run away. When the Moor saw this, he became exceedingly angry. He grabbed the boy in mid-flight and, raising his hand, delivered to Aladdin's head

a blow so hard that it was small wonder his back teeth weren't knocked out.

"O my uncle, what have I done to deserve from thee such a blow as this?" cried Aladdin.

"My son," replied the Magician, "'tis my intent to make thee a man, therefore do not oppose me, for I am thine uncle and like a father unto thee. Obey me in all I bid thee, and shortly thou shalt look upon incredible marvels. Under yon stone lies the treasure I speak of. Only thou hast the power to raise the slab and collect the hoard that lies therein; now go to yonder ring and uplift it as I bid thee."

Aladdin replied, "O uncle of mine, surely it is too heavy for me.

"Nay, my son," answered the Moor. "Put thy hand upon the ring and pull it up, but while lifting repeat thy name and the names of thy father and mother, and it will rise at once."

Aladdin did as he was told, raised the stone, and threw it aside.

"Now, O Aladdin, do whatso I bid thee," said the Magician. "Go down into this vault. When thou reachest the bottom, pass through the four halls containing gold and silver jars. Take care not to touch them. Open the door at the end of the last hall and enter the garden adorned with fruit-bearing trees. Follow the path which leads to an alcove, where thou shalt find a Lamp. Take it and place it in thy breast pocket. Return by the same route, plucking whatso pleases thee from the fruit-bearing trees along the way."

The Moorman then drew a ring from his finger, saying, "Take this ring, O my son. It shall protect thee from all hurt and fear, but only if thou bearest in mind all I have told thee."

Aladdin arose, took the ring, and descended into the cavern, where he found everything just as the Magician had foretold. Doing as he was instructed, he made his way to the alcove containing the Lamp.

Upon his return he marveled at the size and beauty of the fruit on the trees and collected some of each until his pockets were crammed full. He had no idea that the fruits were rare and costly gems, which in color and size surpassed those that any of the Kings of the World had ever owned. After passing through the four halls, he climbed the steps to exit the cave but, being jewel-laden, had difficulty in reaching the top.

"O my uncle," he called, "lend me thy hand and help me out."

The Moorman answered, "O my son, give me the Lamp and lighten thy load."

"The Lamp weighs me down not at all," Aladdin replied, "but do lend me a hand, and as soon as I reach ground I will give it to thee."

The Magician, seeing that Aladdin would hand over the Lamp only upon leaving the cave, became furious and, casting spells and curses over the fire, caused the slab to cover the entrance of the vault and the earth to bury the stone, as it was before.

The Wizard, having lost hope of obtaining the Lamp, returned

to Africa, and Aladdin, unable to issue forth, remained underground in the still and dark cavern.

Now, when Aladdin realized the unhappy calamity that had befallen him, he fell to weeping and wailing, rubbing his hands together in despair. In so doing, his fingers chanced to rub the ring the Magician had given him. At once a fearsome Genie appeared and said, "Behold, I am here! Ask whatsoever thou wantest, for I am the slave to him whose hand bears the Ring."

Aladdin trembled at the terrible sight but, collecting his wits, commanded, "Ho, thou Slave of the Ring, set me upon the face of the earth!"

Hardly had he spoken when the earth opened up and he found himself outside. The lad made his way home and informed his mother of all that had befallen him, weeping all the while.

"O my mother," he cried, "learn that this wretch who tricked us into believing him a concerned and affectionate relation is a Sorcerer, an accursed, and a liar!" After he finished his tale, being hungry, he asked his mother to bring him something to eat.

"O my son," she explained, "I have naught in the house, but I have spun a bit of yarn, which I will sell and then buy some food for thee."

"O my mother," said he, "keep your yarn, but fetch me the Lamp, and I will sell it, for I deem it will bring more money than thy spinnings."

So his mother fetched the Lamp, saying, "It is very dirty. After

we have washed and polished it, perhaps it will sell all the better."

She began to rub the vessel, when suddenly there appeared a Genie of such immense bulk and frightful visage that she quaked in terror and fell into a swoon.

The Genie bellowed in a voice of thunder, "Say whatsoever thou wantest of me! Here am I, the slave to whoso holdeth the Lamp!"

Aladdin snatched the Lamp from his mother and said, "O Slave of the Lamp, I am hungry and desire something to eat."

The Genie disappeared and in the twinkling of an eye returned with a large silver tray bearing golden platters of various meats, delicate dainties, snow-white bread, and two silver cups with as many silver bottles containing sweet and dry wine. Setting these before Aladdin, he vanished from sight.

Aladdin revived his mother, and they sat down to the tray and fell to feeding.

When they had finished the meal, the mother turned to her son and said, "Tell me, O my child, what was that accursed thing who showed himself and nigh unto killed me with fright?"

Aladdin explained the appearance of the Genie of the Lamp as well as that of the Ring. His mother begged him to throw both objects away, as she felt they could do naught but bring misfortune upon herself and her son.

" 'Tis impossible," he replied, "that I part with the Lamp or the Ring. Thou hast seen what good the Slave of the Lamp wrought us when we were famishing, and, yea, but for the Ring, I'd be here not! However, O my mother, in regard to thy feelings, I will

hide away the Lamp and not summon its Spirit in thy presence."

When the food the Genie had brought was gone, Aladdin took the silver tray and golden plates and sold them, one by one, in the Bazaar. In such a manner they continued to be well fed and free from want.

Time and time, the years passed, and Aladdin, having matured, took to frequenting the marketplace and there companying with the various merchants. He learned matters of merchandise, and the twistings and turnings of investments. Eventually he became aware that the tree fruits collected from the enchanted garden were gems of such rare value that he had acquired immense wealth such as Kings can never possess.

One day the Emperor's Herald announced through the streets, "Hear ye! By command of our magnificent master, the King of the Time and Lord of the Age and Tide. Let all the fold lock up their shops and retire within their houses, for the Lady Badr al-budur, daughter of the Emperor, wishes to visit the city. Whosoever disobeys this order shall be punished by death."

Aladdin, having heard of the Lady's great beauty, wished to see her, and hid behind the city gate. When the Princess passed by, Aladdin was struck dumb by her loveliness and grace. Love for her got hold of his heart, and when he returned home he was as one in ecstasy.

His mother, taking note of his strange behavior, queried, "O my

son, what ails thee?" "O my mother," answered the lad, "I am well in body and in no wise ill." He told her of his falling in love with the Lady Badr al-budur and of his resolve to have her for his wife.

"O my child, hast thou gone mad?" cried his mother. "Speak not such things lest anyone think thee insane. Remember thou art a pauper's son. What makes thee think the King of China-land, who has no equal before or behind him, would ever consider giving thee his daughter as wife? Who would dare approach him with such a request? And what gift canst thou submit to the King's Majesty, if indeed an audience is granted?"

"These things I have considered," said Aladdin, "and beg thee to take my request to the Emperor. Also, hear that the tree fruits collected from the treasure cave are the costliest gems. I will fill a porcelain bowl with these jewels, and thou shalt carry it as an offering to the King."

Aladdin's mother reluctantly agreed to do as he asked, and next morning arose, took the bowl full of jewels, which she wrapped in a fine linen kerchief, and went forth to the Palace. She entered the audience chamber, where the King, seated upon his throne and attended by his Ministers, High Officials, and the Grand Wazir, was conducting his business of the day. When all else had been attended to, she at last found herself before the King's Majesty.

"My good woman," he asked, "dost thou have any favor I may grant?"

She bowed low and, after blessing him, answered, "O King of

the Age, I have a request but prefer it to be for thine ears alone."

The Emperor dismissed his entire court save for the Grand Wazir, who held the King's highest confidence.

After begging his pardon for such a bold favor, Aladdin's mother related all regarding her son and his love for the Lady Badr al-budur. The King regarded her with kindness, and laughing, inquired what she carried beneath the kerchief.

Unwrapping the jewel-laden bowl, she presented it to her sovereign. He was dazzled and amazed at the radiance of the gems and exclaimed, "Never until this day saw I anything like these jewels. Indeed, whoso presents to me such gems merits to become bridegroom to my daughter. What say thou, O Wazir?"

The Wazir, hearing the Emperor's words, was exceedingly sorrowful, for it was his design to advance his own child by making him son-in-law to the King. He replied, "Never saw I such gems, O my Lord, but if indeed the sender of this treasure is worthy of the Princess, then let him deliver her forty platters of pure gold, all brimming with jewels, and as many Mameluke slaves to carry them, and let these slaves be escorted by forty handmaidens."

"So be it!" rejoined the Emperor. "If thy son accomplishes this task, I will marry him with my daughter."

Aladdin's mother returned home and related the King's demands to her child, saying, "O my son, he expects of thee an instant reply, but I fancy that we have no answer for him."

Aladdin reassured his worthy parent, then, returning to his chamber, took the Lamp and rubbed it. When the Genie appeared,

he made his request, and in the space of an hour there materialized the platters, jewels, slaves, and handmaidens. Going to his mother, Aladdin bade her go at once to the Palace.

The Mamelukes and maids paced forth in pairs, the gem-laden trays covered with gold-trimmed cloths borne high, and all were followed by Aladdin's mother. Great was the Emperor's joy and wonder, and greater still the surprise and envy of the Wazir when the slaves entered the audience chamber.

The King turned to his minister, saying, "Now, O Wazir, is not he who would produce such wealth in so brief a time worthy to take the King's daughter to wife?" The Wazir could but murmur an assent.

The King then addressed Aladdin's mother: "O good dame, go to thy son and bid him come at once, and this night shall be the beginning of the marriage festivities!"

Aladdin's mother returned home with all speed and told Aladdin her joyous news, adding, "And now, O my son, my job is done; whatsoever happen, the rest is upon thy shoulders."

The young man, thanking her for her labors, kissed her hand, entered his chamber, and once again summoned the Slave of the Lamp.

"Behold, I am here! Ask whatso thou wantest!"

Aladdin replied, "'Tis my desire that thou fetchest me a robe so costly and kingly that no monarch ever owned its like. Also, a stallion fit for the riding of a god, and let its saddle and trappings be of gold crusted with the finest gems. Lastly, I wish attendants to

accompany me, some as body servants, others to scatter gold coins amongst the crowds as I wend my way to the Royal Palace."

"To hear is to obey!" said the Genie, and disappeared. In a moment he was back with all he'd been bidden to bring.

Aladdin put on the robe, mounted the stallion, and, followed by his servants, made his progress through the streets. The slaves threw the coins to the crowd, and one and all marveled at the splendor and generosity of one who until then had been naught but a poor tailor's son.

The Emperor, struck with admiration upon seeing Aladdin in his princely garb, came down from his throne, embraced him, and seated him at his right hand. Refreshments were served, during which Aladdin and his father-in-law-to-be indulged in light conversation and exchanged confidences.

After they had eaten, Aladdin arose and made to leave. The King asked whither he was off, since the marriage contracts were waiting to be signed and the ceremony performed.

The bridegroom replied, "O my Lord the King, 'tis my desire to build for the Lady Badr al-budur a palace befitting her, nor can I marry before so doing. It is also my wish for this palace to be the neighbor of thine own, that I may be nearhand to thy Highness." So saying, he farewelled the King, took horse, and with his slaves returned home.

Going to his chamber, Aladdin rubbed the Lamp, and when the Genie appeared, commanded him to build with all speed a palace

fronting that of the Emperor's, requiring it to be a marvel of marvels, provided with every requisite, such as royal furniture, costly hangings, delicate porcelains, chests full of kingly apparel, the stables to house the swiftest and sleekest of steeds, and the pantries to supply any and all needs. He also wanted a carpet of the richest gold-worked brocade to be stretched from his palace to that of the Emperor's, so that the Lady Badr al-budur might, when coming hither, step upon it and not on common ground.

The Genie departed for a short while and said on his return, "O my lord, that which thou demandest is done."

Imagine the King's delight and surprise when the following morn he glanced from his window and beheld a magnificent palace opposite his. That very evening the marriage ceremony was performed under a silken canopy amidst clouds of perfumed incense. After which one and all celebrated the wedding with merriment and feasting.

Time and time, the years passed, and Aladdin proved himself a generous, wise, and just prince, a shrewd and valiant soldier, the best of loving husbands, and a highly esteemed son-in-law.

Meanwhile in Africa, the wicked Magician discovered, to his vast astonishment, that Aladdin had escaped from the cave and was now enjoying the benefits of the enchanted Lamp. So fierce was his rage that he nearly died of an apoplectic fit. Immediately he set forth for China, where he arrived in due time.

Once there, he disguised himself in beggar's rags and purchased a basket full of brass and copper lamps, then wandered about the city crying, "Ho! Who will exchange old lamps for new?" This drew forth taunts and laughter from the town folk, who thought him mad for offering new for old.

When he reached the courtyard of Aladdin's palace, the Princess, hearing the commotion, sent one of her maids-in-waiting to see what it was about. The girl returned, laughing, and as loudly laughed the Princess when this strange tale was told to her. Now, Aladdin had gone hunting for a few days and had carelessly left the Lamp in his chamber without hiding it.

One of the slave girls who had seen it said, "O my Lady, I think to have noticed in the chamber of my Lord, Aladdin, an old lamp. Let us try to exchange it and see if this madman's cry be truth or lie."

The Princess readily agreed, thinking the episode a pleasant joke to relate to her husband upon his return.

When the exchange had been made, the Moroccan, recognizing the enchanted vessel, threw down the other lamps and went forth running till he was clear of the city.

That evening he rubbed the Lamp, summoned its Genie, and commanded that he and Aladdin's palace with all therein be transported to his own land of Africa. "I hear and obey!" thundered the Slave of the Lamp, and in an eye-twinkling it was done. Such then was the work of the Moorman, the Magician.

But now let us return to the Emperor and his son-in-law. It was the custom of the King upon rising in the morning to look out his window that he might catch sight of his beloved daughter's abode. Great was his amazement when he did so the next dawn. He was bewildered and rubbed his eyes, thinking they were playing tricks upon him. At last realizing that indeed the palace and all therein had vanished, he summoned the Grand Wazir and demanded, "Where be Aladdin?"

"He has gone a-hunting," was the reply.

The King raged and ordered his army officers to go without delay and bring his son-in-law to him in chains.

When Aladdin appeared before the Emperor, he asked, "O my Lord, inasmuch as thy Highness has favored me till now, what have I done to merit such treatment?"

"O traitor," cried the King, "look out the window and tell us where is thy palace, and where is my daughter, the core of my heart and my only child?" The Prince obeyed the command and was astonished and perplexed at seeing a vast empty plain where once his palace had stood.

"O King of the Age," he said, "I know not what hath befallen."

"Thou must know, O Aladdin," the Emperor rejoined. "I will pardon thee only that thou go and look into this affair and find my daughter. Do not ever show thyself in my presence without her; and if thou findest her not, then by all that is holy, I will cut off thy head!"

Aladdin replied, "To hear is to obey: If after seven days I fail

to find and fetch thy daughter, my wife, strike off my head and do with me whatso thou wishest."

So he went forth a-wandering about the capital for two days, knowing not where nor how to begin his search. On the third day he strayed aimlessly about the open wastelands outlying the city walls. Wringing his hands in despair and sorrow, Aladdin happened to rub the magic Ring he wore on his finger.

Instantly the Genie appeared: "Behold, the Slave between thy hands is here, ask of me whatso thou wantest!"

Seeing the Genie, Aladdin cried, "O Slave, I desire thee to bring before me my wife and my palace together with all and everything it contains."

The Spirit replied that only the Slave of the Lamp could perform such a task. He could, however, set the Prince down beside his palace in whatever land it might be.

"So be it!" Aladdin commanded. The Genie lifted him high in the air and in a matter of seconds set him down in the land of Africa, upon a spot facing his wife's chamber.

When the Lady Badr al-budur happened to glance out her window and saw her husband, she was filled with joy and bade him enter at once. After many tender embraces and tears of happiness at being reunited, Aladdin asked the Princess as to the whys and wherefores of her present situation.

She told him of how the accursed Magician had obtained the enchanted Lamp, which he carried on his person at all times,

and then spirited the palace to Africa. Now he was trying to force her to take him as husband in Aladdin's place. This he swore to accomplish by the power of magic, if necessary. She had been able to repulse these unwanted threats and advances because her fear and hatred of the evil Moor were as strong as her love and respect were for Aladdin.

"O Spawn of Hell!" cried Aladdin. "If thou wert before me, I'd clasp my hands about thy wretched throat and squeeze the worthless life from thy body!" After he vented his rage, heaping numerous oaths and curses upon the Moorman, the Prince turned to his wife and said, "O my Lady, do thus listen, and most carefully, to me. Do exactly as I bid thee, for our future happiness depends upon it.

"When the accursed one comes to woo thee, appear before him in thy most costly and bewitching apparel, and receive him with a greeting of 'Welcome and fair welcome.' Pour honeylike words into his ears and cast longing glances in his direction. Whilst intoxicating his senses, do thou the same with his thirst. He cannot but help be robbed of his wits, and in his delight will be as clay in thy hands. When he seems besotted with drink and love, pour this potion into his wine and bid him drink yet again. It shall be for the last time: no sooner shall he drink of it than he will fall in a fit upon his back and die. I will be in thine antechamber. When all is done, come unto me, and I will dispose of the rest." Aladdin then gave his wife the vial of poison and, taking leave of her, went into the other room.

And so the Lady Badr al-budur summoned her serving maid and prepared herself for the Moroccan's visit. When he at last entered, she did as Aladdin bade her, and the Moor, taken with her dazzling appearance and seductive manner, was soon drunk with love and wine. Supper was served, during which the Princess beguiled the Magician by addressing him in the sweetest terms. The Moor's longing for her increased, and when they had come to the last of the supper and the wine had mastered his brain, the Princess said, "There is a custom throughout our country, but I know not if it be of usage in yours."

The Moorman replied, "And what may that be?"

So she said to him, "At the end of supper, each partner takes the cup of the beloved and drinks thereof."

Then, filling her cup with wine, and secretly slipping the poison into it, she passed it to the Magician, taking his in return. "O my life," she murmured, "here is thy cup with me, and my cup with thee, and in China-land thus do lovers drink to one another." She kissed the rim of his cup and drank from it, throwing loving glances in his direction all the while.

In delirious joy, the Wizard raised her cup to his lips and drank off the poisoned draught at once. Immediately he jumped from his seat and, staggering backward, fell dead at her feet.

The Princess ran hurriedly into the antechamber and Aladdin's arms. He bade her remain and, returning to the dining room, walked up to the Moorman's body and drew from his breast pocket the Magic Lamp. He rubbed the Lamp; the Genie appeared

and asked, "I am here, O my Lord. What is it thou wantest?"

"I wish," answered Aladdin, "that thou takest up my palace from this country and transport it to the land of China, and set it down upon its original site, facing the palace of the Emperor."

The Slave replied, "I hear and obey!" And so it was done.

As regards the Emperor: After he drove away his son-in-law, he never ceased to sorrow for the loss of his daughter, and each morning, when he arose, would go to his window and peer in the direction where formerly Aladdin's palace had stood. Now, on that day, when he looked out the window, lo and behold, he saw an edifice where before had been nothing! After rubbing his eyes to be sure they weren't playing tricks upon him, the Emperor called for a horse and, without delay, mounted and made for the palace. When Aladdin saw his father-in-law approaching, he went down to greet him.

Taking his hand, he led the King to the apartment of his daughter, where a joyous reunion took place. The Princess repeated to her father everything that had happened to her, concluding with the arrival of Aladdin, the death of the wicked Moor, and their return to the land of China. The King ordered the Magician's carcass burned and its ashes scattered to the wind. After which a holiday was declared in honor of the Lady Badr al-budur and Aladdin's safe return, and the feasting and rejoicing lasted for thirty days.

Thence forward Aladdin and his wife lived in all pleasure and joy, raising numerous offspring to the delight of the old King.

Time and time, and when the Emperor deceased, his son-in-law was seated upon the throne of the kingdom, and he ruled with such wisdom and justice that all the fold loved and respected him.

The years passed in solace and happiness, and destiny endowed Aladdin and his family with days the most delectable, and they had the lifeliest of lives until, at last, there came to them the Destroyer of Delights, and Sunderer of Societies, and they became as though they never had been, and were at rest.

ABOUT THE BOOK

Leonard Lubin writes, "The artwork for *Aladdin and His Wonderful Lamp* was done in pencil on Bristol paper (plate finish). It is in the French Chinoiserie manner, influenced by the drawings of J. B. Pillemont. He was an eighteenth-century decorative artist who developed and helped spread the rococo Chinoiserie style throughout Europe.

"Also, I must refer to Frederick Crace, designer of much of the interior of the Brighton Pavilion (the seaside pleasure dome of George IV), which, as far as I'm concerned, was, and is, the most flamboyant and opulent expression of the Chinoiserie craze."

The text type used in *Aladdin and His Wonderful Lamp* is Perpetua. The book was printed by Princeton Polychrome Press and bound by A. Horowitz & Sons.